Korean Nursery Rhymes

Wild Geese, Land of Goblins

and Other Favorite Songs and Rhymes

Danielle Wright

Illustrated by

Helen Acraman

TUTTLE Publishing

Tokyo | Rutland, Vermont | Singapore

Contents

Introduction   3

Butterfly   by Unknown   5

Little One   by traditional song   6

Our House   by traditional song   8

Island Baby   by In-hyeon Han   10

Here, There   by Suk-kyeong Kim   12

Land of Goblins   by Unknown   14

Monkey's Bottom   by traditional song   16

Cotton Candy   by Geun Jeong   18

Wild Geese   by traditional song   21

Spring in My Hometown   by Weon-su Yi   22

Twirling Round   by traditional song   24

Little Fox   by traditional song   26

Half Moon   by Geuk-yeong Yun   28

Land of White   by Seong-gyun Kim   31

Translations by Jenny Wang Medina and Binna Lee, except for "Here, There!" and "Cotton Candy," also with help from Stephen Epstein. Additional translation support and cultural assistance from Paul and Yvonne Jeong. Edited by Danielle Wright. Thanks to Jenny Wang Medina for additional research and help with KOMCA clearances. Tranliterations of these rhumes adhere to the Revised Romanization System of Korean.

Introduction

Where in the world would you find a potty training rhyme about a monkey's bottom and the weird and wonderful shapes its poo makes? For me, it could only be Korea. This is just one of many rhymes that capture a childlike side to Korean culture that is fun-loving and original.

Many of the rhymes I have chosen involve children singing together or with their parents. For example, "Here, There" is a lovely rhyme for a mother and child to sing to each other. Others, like "Our House" and "Little One" get children up and moving, with so many of these rhymes involving collaboration, some even ending with a "Rock, Paper, Scissors" game to decide who will be out or in for the next round.

I also found beautiful lullabies in Korean. One of my all-time favorites is "Island Baby," which speaks to the modern reader, yet is steeped in history. Others, like "Spring in my Hometown," carry a theme common in many international collections of nursery rhymes – a love for what we call "the green grass of home."

Lovely young voices sing all the songs in both Korean and English on the accompanying CD. For the Korean language versions, we have kept the focus on the language itself, but the English language versions demonstrate the call-and-response nature of many of the rhymes.

The Korean national writing system is called Hanguel and is written with spaces between words, a feature not found in Chinese or Japanese. Traditionally, Korean was written in columns, but now is usually written in rows—from left to right, top to bottom.

Recently, I read a sign on a blackboard outside a café in Auckland with the words: "We all smile in the same language." North and South Koreans also share the same spoken language, although each calls it by a different name—Hangungmal in South Korea, and Chosŏnmal in North Korea. Hopefully, this common language bond and the rhymes they once shared as children will, one day, bring them together again.

I hope you enjoy reading and listening to these favorite Korean rhymes.

With best wishes,
Danielle Wright
www.itsasmallworld.co.nz

Butterfly

나비야 나비야
Nabiya nabiya

나비야 나비야 이리날아 오너라
Nabiya, nabiya iri-nara oneora
Butterfly, butterfly, won't you come and play with me?

노랑나비 흰나비 춤을 추며 오너라
Norang nabi huin-nabi chum-eul chu-myeo oneora
White and yellow butterflies, won't you come and dance with me?

봄바람에 꽃잎도 방긋방긋 웃으며
Bombaram-e kkotipdo bang-geut bang-geut useumyeo
Flower petals in the breeze, smiling brightly 'cause it's spring

참새도 짹짹짹 노래하며 춤춘다
Chamsae-do jjaek-jjaek-jjaek noraehamyeo chumchunda
Sparrows chirping - chirp chirp chirp - dancing to a merry song

Little One
꼬마야 꼬마야
Kkomaya kkomaya

꼬마야 꼬마야 뒤로 돌아라
Kkomaya kkomaya dui-ro dorara
Little one, little one, turn around

꼬마야 꼬마야 한발을 들어라
Kkomaya kkomaya hanbal-eul deureo-ra
Little one, little one, lift one leg up

꼬마야 꼬마야 땅을 짚어라
Kkomaya kkomaya ttang-eul jipeora
Little one, little one, hand upon the floor

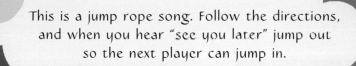

This is a jump rope song. Follow the directions, and when you hear "see you later" jump out so the next player can jump in.

꼬마야 꼬마야 손벽릉 쳐라
Kkomaya kkomaya sonbyeog-reung chyeora
Little one, little one, clap your hands

꼬마야 꼬마야 만세를 불러라
Kkomaya kkomaya manse-reul bulleo-ra
Little one, little one, raise your hands up

꼬마야 꼬마야 잘 가거라
Kkomaya kkomaya jal gageora
Little one, little one, see you later

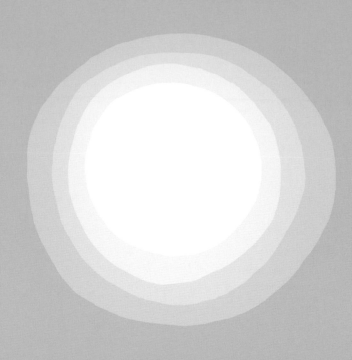

Our House
우리집에 왜 왔니
Uri jip

우리집에 왜 왔니 왜 왔니 왜 왔니
Uri jip-e wae wassni wae wassni wae wassni
Why have you come to our house, our house, our house?

꽃 찾으러 왔단다 왔단다 왔단다
Kkoch chajeureo wassdanda wassdanda wassdanda
I've come to pick some flowers, flowers, flowers

This is a "call and response" game played with two teams. Team members stand shoulder to shoulder and hold hands. The two groups face each other, walking forwards when they are singing, and backwards when they're being sung to. At the end of the round a game of Rock Paper Scissors decides which team gets to take a member of the other team for the next round.

무슨 꽃을 찾으러 왔느냐 왔느냐
Museun kkoch-eul chajeureo wassneunya wassneunya
Which ones will you take with you, take with you, take with you?

진달래 꽃을 찾으러 왔단다 왔단다 왔단다*
Jindallae kkocheul chajeureo wassdanda wassdanda wassdanda
I've come to pick azaleas, azaleas, azaleas

가위 바위 보!
Kawi bawi bo!
Rock, paper, scissors!

*Or substitute any
flower you like.

Island Baby
섬집아기
Seomijp agi

엄마가 섬그늘에 굴 따러가면
Eomma-ga seomgeuneul-e gul ttara-gamyeon
Off a shady cove, mommy picks oysters

아기가 혼자남아 집을 보다가
Agi-ga honja-nama jipeul bodaga
Watching over the home, baby's all alone

바다가 들려주는 자장노래에
Bada-ga deulryeo-juneon jajangnorae-e
Ocean is singing to her, a lulling lullaby

팔 베고 스르르르 잠이 돕니다
Pal bego seu-reureureu jam-i deubnida
Resting her head on her arms, drifting off to sleep

아기는 잠을곤히 자고있지만
Agi-neun jameulgon-hi jago-issjiman
Though baby's fast asleep, sound asleep in bed

갈매기 울음소리 맘이 설레어
Galmaegi ureumsori mam-i seolle-eo
Seagull's cries pull on mom's heartstrings, calling her home

다 못찬 굴 바구니 머리에 이고
Da motchan gul baguni meori-e igo
She lifts her half-full basket, up above her head

엄마는 모갯길을 달려옵니다
Eomma-neun moraetgil-eul dalyeo-obnida
Chasing the sandy path, Mommy's coming home

달려 옵니다
Dalyeo-obnida
Mommy's coming home

Here, There
요기 여기
Yogi Yeogi

눈은 어디 있나, 요기
Nun eun eodi issna, yogi
Where are my eyes? Here!

코는 어디 있나, 요기
Ko neun eodi issna, yogi
Where is my nose? Here!

귀는 어디 있나, 요기
Gwi neun eodi issna, yogi
Where are my ears? Here!

입은 어디 있을까, 요기
Ip-eun eodi isseul-kka yogi
What about my mouth? Here!

엄마 눈은 어디 있나, 여기
Eomma nun eun eodi issna, yeogi
Where are Mommy's eyes? There!

엄마 코는 어디 있나, 여기
Eomma ko neun eodi issna, yeogi
Where is Mommy's nose? There!

엄마 귀는 어디 있나, 여기
Eomma gwi neun eodi issna, yeogi
Where are Mommy's ears? There!

입은 어디 있을까, 여기
Ip-eun eodi isseul-kka, yeogi
What about Mommy's mouth? There!

The child will first point to his or her own features, then to Mommy's in this rhyme created for mother and child to play together.

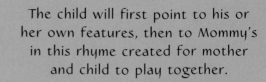

Land of Goblins
도깨비 나라
Dokkaebi nara

In Korean folklore, goblins live in the mountains and are mischievous creatures. This song refers to a folktale where a poor man comes upon a goblin house and uses their magic clubs to turn things to gold and silver.

14

이상하고 아름다운 도깨비 나라
Isang-hago areum-daun dokkaebi nara
Strange and beautiful land of goblins—have you ever been?

방망이를 두드리면 무엇이 될까
Bangmangi-reul dudeuri-myeon mu-eosi doelkka?
When the goblin bangs his magic club what will it bring?

금 나와라 와라 뚝딱
Geum nawara wara ttukttak
Gold, come out, out, chop and crack!

은 나와라 와라 뚝딱
Eun nawara wara ttukttak
Silver, come out, out, chop and crack!

Monkey's Bottom
원숭이 엉덩이
Weonsungi eongdeongi

원숭이 엉덩이는 빨개
Weonsungi eongdeongi-neun ppalgae
Monkey's bottom's red

빨가면 사과
Ppalgamyeon sagwa
If it's red, apple

사과는 맛있어
Sagwaneun massisseo
Apples are yummy

맛있으면 바나나
Massisseumyeon banana
If it's yummy, banana

바나나는 길어
Banana-neun gireo
Bananas are long

길면 기차
Gilmyeon gicha
If it's long, choo choo train

기차는 빨라
Gicha-neun ppalla
Choo choo trains are fast

빠르면 비행기
Ppareumyeon bihaenggi
If it's fast, airplane

비행기는 높아
Bihaenggi-neun nopa
Airplanes fly high

높으면 백두산
Nopeumyeon Paekdusan
If it's high, Mount Paekdu!

Children and parents commonly sing this rhyme together. Parents start the line, and children finish it. This rhyme is used to help children learn about using the potty, and the shapes poo makes, but it's also a great song about how one thought leads to another. Mount Paekdu is a sacred mountain on the Northeastern part of the Korean peninsula.

Cotton Candy
솜사탕
Somsatang

Cotton Candy (also known as Candy Floss) is very popular in Korea and, like in the U.S. and elsewhere, it comes in lots of colors—not just white.

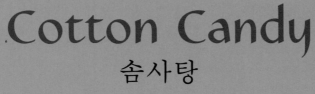

18

나뭇가지에 실처럼 날아든 솜사탕
Namugaji-e sil-cheoreom naradeun somsatang
Cotton candy caught on a branch like thread

하얀 눈처럼 희고도 깨끗한 솜사탕
Hayan nun-cheoreom huigodo kkaekkeut-han somsatang
Fluffy white cotton candy just like white snow

엄마 손잡고 나들이할 때 먹어본 솜사탕
Eomma son-jabgo nadeuri-hal ttae meogeo-bon somsatang
I had it once before, holding Mommy's hand

훅훅 불면은 구멍이 뚫리는 커다란 솜사탕
Huk-huk bulmyeon-eun gumeong-i ttulhli-neun keodaran somsatang
Puffy cotton candy you can blow a hole right through

This song is done with hand gestures, similar to
"Patty-cake," and like many Korean rhymes, ends
in the "Rock, Paper, Scissors" game. The goose
reminds the children of their teacher, who is away.
They hope to hear lots of news from their teacher.

Wild Geese

기러기
Kireogi

아침 바람 찬 바람에, 울고 가는 저 기러기
Achim baram chan baram-e, ulgo ganeun jeo gireogi
A goose flies in the cold morning wind

우리선생 계실 적에, 엽서 한장 써주세요
Uri-seonsaeng gyesil jeok-e, yeopseo hanjang sseo-juseyo
Teacher, while you're gone please write us a postcard

한장 말고 두 장이요, 두 장 말고 세 장이요
Hanjang malgo du jangiyo, du jang malgo se jangiyo
Not one but two postcards, not two but three postcards

구리 구리 구리 구리 가위, 바위, 보!
Guri guri guri guri gawi, bawi, bo!
Round and round and round and round and rock, paper, scissors!

Spring in My Hometown

고향의 봄

Gohyang ui bom

나의 살던 고향은 꽃피는 산골

Na-ui saldeon gohyang-eun kkotpi-neun sangol

Flowers bloom in my hometown, a hamlet in the hills

복숭아꽃 살구꽃 아기 진달래

Boksunga-kkoch salgu-kkoch agi jindallae

Little azaleas, peach flowers, apricot blossoms

울긋불긋 꽃 대궐 차리인 동네

Ulgeut-bulgeut kkoch daegwol chari-in dongne

Blooming colors through the village, a flowery palace

그 속 에서 놀던 때가 그립습니다

Geu sok-eseo noldeon ttaega geurip-seupnida

Longing for my sweet hometown, where I used to play

꽃 동네 새 동네 나의 옛 고향

Kkoch dongne sae dongne na-ui yet gohyang

Birds and blooms in my hometown, long, long time ago

파란들 남쪽에서 바람이 불면

Paran-deul namjjok-eseo barami bulmyeon

Soft breezes from the south blowing over green fields

냇가에 수양버들 춤추는 동네

Naetga-e suyangbeo-deul chumchu-neun dongne

Weeping willow dancing by the stream through my village

그 속에서 놀던 때가 그립습니다

Geu sok-eseo noldeon ttaega geuripseupnida

Longing for my sweet hometown where I used to play

Twirling Round
뱅글뱅글 돌아서
Baeng-geul baeng-geul doraseo

올라간 머리 내려온 머리
Ollagan meori naeryeo-on meori
Hair goes up, hair goes down

뱅글뱅글 돌아서 도깨비 머리
Baeng-geul baeng-geul doraseo dokkaebi meori
Twirling, twirling, round and round, making goblin horns

올라간 눈 내려온 눈
Ollagan nun naeryeo-on nun
Eyes go up, eyes go down

뱅글뱅글 돌아서 고양이 눈
Baeng-geul baeng-geul doraseo goyangi nun
Twirling, twirling, round and round, making kitty eyes

올라간 코 내려온 코
Ollagan ko naeryeo-on ko
Nose goes up, nose goes down

뱅글뱅글 돌아서 돼지 코
Baeng-geul baeng-geul doraseo dwaeji ko
Twirling, twirling, round and round, making piggy snout

올라간 입 내려간 입
Ollagan ip naeryeo-gan ip
Mouth goes up, mouth goes down

뱅글뱅글 돌아서 붕어 입
Baeng-geul baeng-geul doraseo bung-eo ip
Twirling, twirling, round and round, making fishy face

Children use their hands to make the faces described in this song, like pushing up their noses to make piggy snouts.

Little Fox
여우야, 여우야
Yeo-uya, yeo-uya

여우야 여우야 뭐하니?
Yeo-uya, yeo-uya mueoha-ni?
Little fox, little fox, what do you do?

잠잔다.
Jam-janda
I'm sleeping

잠꾸러기!
Jamkkureogi!
Sleepy head!

여우야 여우야 뭐하니?
Yeo-uya yeo-uya mueoha-ni?
Little fox, little fox, what do you do?

세수한다.
Sesu-handa
I'm washing up

멋장이!
Meot-jangi!
Handsome lad!

This game is part of a game like "Duck Duck Goose." Everyone sits in a circle and the person who is "it" goes around the outside of the circle, tapping each person on the head. The last person to be tapped gets to decide whether to shout "Go!" or "Stay!"

여우야 여우야 뭐하니?
Yeo-uya yeo-uya mueoha-ni?
Little fox, little fox, what do you do?

밥 먹는다.
Bab meoknunda
I'm eating rice

무슨반찬?
Museun banchan?
With what on the side?

개구리 반찬
Gaeguri banchan
Frog on the side

죽었니? 살았니?
Jugeossni? Sarassni?
Did you go? Did you stay?

죽었다!/살았다!
Jukeoss-da!/Sarass-da!
Go!/Stay!

Half Moon
반달
Ban-dal

In Asian cultures the man in the moon
isn't a man at all, but a rabbit. To Koreans
the shadow on the moon looks like a rabbit
who is pounding rice to make rice cakes.

푸른 하늘 은하수 하얀 쪽 배엔
Pureun haneul eun-hasu hayan jjok bae-en
In a small white boat, sailing across the Milky Way

계수나무 한 나무 토끼 한 마리
Gyesu namu han namu tokki han mari
White rabbit is all alone with his laurel tree

돛대도 아니 달고 삿대도 없이
Doch-daedo ani dalgo satdaedo eopsi
Without sail and without oar

가기도 잘도간다 서쪽 나라로
Gagido jal-do ganda seojjok nara-ro
He glides to a western shore

은하수를 건너서 구름나라로
Eun-hasurul geonneo-seo gureum nara-ro
Across the Milky Way to the land of clouds

구름나라 지나선 어디로 가나
Gureum nara jinaseon eodiro gana
Onward through the mist, heading who knows where

멀리서 반짝반짝 비치이는 건
Meolliseo banjjak-banjjak bichi-ineun geon
Twinkle, twinkle, morning star, gleaming from afar

샛별이 등대란다 길을 찾아라
Saetbyeoli deungdae-randa gileul chajara
Shine, shining lighthouse star, leading the way back home

Land of White
하얀 나라
Hayan nara

나는 눈이 좋아서 꿈에 눈이 오나 봐
Naneun nun-i johaseo kkum-e nun-i ona bwa
I like snow the most of all, snow is falling in my dreams

온 세상이 모두 하얀 나라였지 어젯밤 꿈 속에
On sesang-i modu hayan nara-yeossji eojetbam kkum sok-e
Everything around me, land of white surrounds me in my sweet dreams last night

썰매를 탔죠 눈싸움 했죠 커다란 눈사람도 만들었죠
Sseolmae-rul tassjyo nunssa-um haessjyo keodaran nunsaramdo mandeul-eossjyo
First I rode a sled, had a snowball fight, and then I made a giant snowman

나는 눈이 좋아서 꿈에 눈이 오나 봐
Naneun nun-i johaseo kkum-e nun-i ona bwa
I like snow the most of all, snow is falling in my dreams

온 세상이 모두 하얀 나라였지 어젯밤 꿈 속에
On sesang-i modu hayan narayeossji eojetbam kkum sok-e
Everything around me, land of white surrounds me in my sweet dreams last night

31

The Tuttle Story: "Books to Span the East and West"

Most people are surprised to learn that the world's largest publisher of books on Asia had its humble beginnings in the tiny American state of Vermont. The company's founder, Charles E. Tuttle, belonged to a New England family steeped in publishing. And his first love was naturally books—especially old and rare editions.

Immediately after WW II, serving in Tokyo under General Douglas MacArthur, Tuttle was tasked with reviving the Japanese publishing industry. He later founded the Charles E. Tuttle Publishing Company, which thrives today as one of the world's leading independent publishers.

Though a westerner, Tuttle was hugely instrumental in bringing a knowledge of Japan and Asia to a world hungry for information about the East. By the time of his death in 1993, Tuttle had published over 6,000 books on Asian culture, history and art—a legacy honored by the Japanese emperor with the "Order of the Sacred Treasure," the highest tribute Japan can bestow upon a non-Japanese.

With a backlist of 1,500 titles, Tuttle Publishing is more active today than at any time in its past—inspired by Charles Tuttle's core mission to publish fine books to span the East and West and provide a greater understanding of each.

Published by Tuttle Publishing, an imprint of Periplus Editions (HK) Ltd.

www.tuttlepublishing.com

Library of Congress Cataloging-in-Publication Data

Wright, Danielle.
  Korean nursery rhymes : Wild geese, Land of goblins and other favorite songs and rhymes / by Danielle Wright ; illustrated by Helen Acraman. -- 1st ed.
      v. cm.
  Summary: An illustrated collection of fourteen nursery rhymes, plus notes on Korean culture and explanations of how the jump rope and hand clap games are played. Presented in Hanguel script, Romanized Korean, and English; accompanying CD contains recordings of all of the rhymes performed in Korean and English.
  Contents: Butterfly -- Little one (traditional song) -- Our house (traditional song) -- Island baby / In-hyeon Han -- Here, there / Suk-kyeong Kim -- Land of goblins -- Monkey's bottom (traditional song) -- Cotton candy / Geun Jeong -- Wild Geese (traditional song) -- Spring in my hometown / by Weon-su Yi -- Twirling round (traditional song) -- Little fox (traditional song) -- Half moon / by Geuk-yeong Yun -- Land of white / by Seong-gyun Kim.
  ISBN 978-0-8048-4227-3 (hardback)
1. Nursery rhymes, Korean. 2. Children's poetry, Korean. [1. Nursery rhymes. 2. Korean language materials--Bilingual.] I. Acraman, Helen, ill. II. Title.
  PL975.7.C55W75 2013
  398.809519--dc23
                    2012029066

ISBN 978-0-8048-4227-3

Distributed by

North America, Latin America & Europe
Tuttle Publishing, 364 Innovation Drive, North Clarendon, VT 05759-9436 U.S.A. Tel: 1 (802) 773-8930; Fax: 1 (802) 773-6993
info@tuttlepublishing.com; www.tuttlepublishing.com

Japan
Tuttle Publishing, Yaekari Bldg., 3rd Floor, 5-4-12 Osaki, Shinagawa-ku, Tokyo 141-0032. Tel: (81) 3 5437-0171; Fax: (81) 3 5437-0755
sales@ tuttle.co.jp; www.tuttle.co.jp

Asia Pacific
Berkeley Books Pte. Ltd., 61 Tai Seng Avenue #02-12, Singapore 534167. Tel: (65) 6280-1330; Fax: (65) 6280-6290
inquiries@periplus.com.sg; www.periplus.com

First edition   16 15 14 13 12   5 4 3 2 1   1211EP   Printed in Hong Kong

TUTTLE PUBLISHING® is a registered trademark of Tuttle Publishing, a division of Periplus Editions (HK) Ltd.

Guide to the CD

Butterfly
lyricist and composer unknown
Sung in English by Jessica Rogers

Little One
traditional song
composer unknown
Sung in English by Maya Rogers

Our House
traditional song
composer unknown
Sung in English by Jessica and Maya Rogers

Island Baby
lyricist In-hyeon Han
composer Hong-cheol Yi
Sung in English by Jessica Rogers

Here, There
lyricist and composer Suk-kyeong Kim
Sung in English by Jessica and Maya Rogers

Land of Goblins
lyricist unknown
composer Tae-jun Pak
Sung in English by Jessica Rogers

Monkey's Bottom
traditional song
composer Unknown
Sung in English by Jessica Rogers,
Maya Rogers and Henry Wright

Cotton Candy
lyricist Geun Jeong
composer Su-in Yi
Sung in English by Jessica Rogers

Wild Geese
traditional song
composer unknown
Sung in English by Jessica Rogers

Spring in My Hometown
lyricist Weon-su Yi
composer Nan-pa Hong
Sung in English by Jessica Rogers

Twirling Round
traditional song
composer unknown
Sung in English by Jessica Rogers

Little Fox
traditional song
composer unknown
Sung in English by Jessica and Maya Rogers

Half Moon
lyricist and composer Geuk-yeong Yun
Sung in English by Jessica Rogers

Land of White
lyricist and composer Seong-gyun Kim
Sung in English by Jessica Rogers

All music arranged and performed by Alex Borwick, borwick.alex@gmail.com
All Korean versions sung by Ah Young Jeong
Recorded and mixed by Steve Garden
Executive produced by Danielle Wright